W9-BLY-978

Julie Andrews Edwards & Emma Walton Hamilton

Dumpy
and the Big Storm

Illustrated by Tony Walton

Hyperion Books for Children/New York

R-R-RUMBLE-TUMBLE-GRUMBLE! The sound
of thunder rolled across the little village of Apple Harbor.

"We're in for a big storm," said Pop-Up to his grandson, Charlie
Barnes, as they were driving home from school. Dumpy, their sturdy
little dump truck, strained against the wind as leaves swirled and did
cartwheels along the streets.

The sheets on Mrs. Penny's laundry line billowed in all directions.

"Look!" Charlie pointed as one escaped its wooden pins and soared high across the rooftops.

"Better get Dumpy into the barn," said Pop-Up. "This could last all night and cause all kinds of damage."

As they drove into Merryhill Farm, preparations for the storm were under way. Mrs. Barnes closed the farmhouse shutters tight. **"BEEP! BEEP! BEEP!"** Bee-Bee the Backhoe said as she stacked the young trees for planting safely against the barn. "Two hands are better than one!"

Farmer Barnes was bringing Trundle the Tractor in from the fields.

"**PUTT-PUTT-PUTT-PUTT!**" said Trundle as he backed into the shed. "All in a day's work!"

Even the old rooster on the barn roof flapped down from his perch to hustle the hens into the chicken coop.

By nightfall, the storm had arrived. Dumpy was glad he was tucked among the warm bales of hay and sweet-smelling apples and potatoes. The rain hammered on the timbers above him, and the large beams creaked and groaned.
WHOOO-HOOO! the wind howled, late into the night.

ZZZIP! There was a bright flash of lightning, followed by a sharp **CLA-A-P!** of thunder.

Up at the farmhouse, Charlie awoke with a start.

WHAP-CLUNK! WHAP-CLUNK! Something was banging noisily in the storm, and he scrambled to the window to see what it was.

"You okay, pal?" Pop-Up stuck his head around the door. "That was a little loud, even for me!"

"The barn door blew open!" Charlie said. "Everything inside will get wet!"

"I'll take care of it!" said Pop-Up.

There was another **CRA-A-CK!** of thunder, and Charlie leaped for his galoshes.

"I'm coming with you!" he said hurriedly.

They braved their way through the slanting rain and buffeting wind, and were struggling to close the barn doors when they heard a strange **CRACKLING** noise coming from Dumpy.

"DRAT!" yelled Pop-Up. "We must have left the radio on!"

"No, we turned it off!" Charlie shouted back.

"Well, maybe it was the lightning," Pop-Up hollered. "But it's going to drain the battery!"

They sloshed into the barn, and just as Pop-Up reached for the radio, the static cleared, and a voice came through:

This is a marine craft warning!" it announced. "Apple Harbor lighthouse has been struck by lightning! Power is down; the lamp and foghorn are disabled. To repeat . . .'"

"They're going to want help," Pop-Up said quickly. "We'd better go wake your dad."

They splashed back to the house. Minutes later a concerned Mrs. Barnes was filling thermoses with hot soup as the men packed up flashlights, rope, chains, blankets, and all kinds of emergency gear.

"Are you sure it's safe for Charlie to go with you?" she asked.

"I have to go, Mom!" Charlie said. "They need *all* the guys!"

"He'll be safe with us, Winnie," Farmer Barnes reassured her. "And it's good experience."

The wind and rain pummeled Dumpy as they set out from
the farm. Farmer Barnes leaned forward for a better view as
Dumpy's wipers whipped back and forth in an attempt to clear
the windshield.

"Better take it slow," Pop-Up cautioned. "Can't see a foot in
front of us!"

"There's something up ahead!" Charlie cried.

Dumpy plowed his way into a patch of flooded road as a large mass loomed out of the downpour.

"It's Stinky the Garbage Truck!" exclaimed Charlie.

"Need some help, Ralph?" yelled Farmer Barnes.

"Engine's waterlogged!" Stinky's driver called back.

"Hold on! We'll get you going again!"

Farmer Barnes found jumper cables, and the men connected them to the two trucks. Dumpy looked at his old friend with concern.

Pop-Up yelled for Charlie to gun Dumpy's engine.

"**BRROOOM! BRROOOM!**" Dumpy roared, and was relieved when Stinky sputtered into life. Farmer Barnes told Ralph about the trouble at the lighthouse, and Ralph immediately responded, "We'll come with you, of course!"

Stinky and Dumpy eased out of the floodwater. Bracing themselves, they set off in the storm once again, glad of each other's company.

They had barely gone half a mile when Tommy the Tow Truck appeared through the sheets of rain. He was struggling to clear a large tree that had fallen and was blocking the road.

"Need a hand, Mr. O'Malley?" Charlie shouted out the window.

"Sure do!" said Tommy's driver gratefully.

Farmer Barnes hooked a strong chain to Dumpy and wrapped it around the tree trunk.

"Clear to go!" he signaled.

"CHUGGA-CHUGGA-CHUG!"
Tommy groaned.
"When they're *down*, I pick 'em *up*!"
"**BRROOOM! BRROOOM!**" Dumpy's wheels fought for
traction in the mud.

The wet and heavy log began to scrape clear of the road, and
Stinky followed, cleaning up the debris.

"**ERR-RNN!**" he said as he crunched the remaining leaves and
branches. "It's not *what* you do, it's *how* you do it!"

When Mr. O'Malley heard about the lighthouse, he quickly signed on to help. There were now three trucks in the rescue party, but just around the corner was yet another challenge.

Big Red the Fire Engine was parked in front of Buttercup Cottage. Fireman Tony was trying to soothe Miss Morris, the librarian, who was rain-soaked and upset. At least a dozen pigs and piglets were tearing around her front lawn, trampling her petunias and wallowing in the mud.

"Those are Pickwick's pigs!" declared Pop-Up. Dumpy skidded to a halt, and the others followed suit.

"They got spooked by the storm and escaped from the farm," Fireman Tony explained as everyone jumped out to help. He handed a wet piglet to Charlie and dove for another. "How am I going to get 'em back? There's no room in a fire truck for pigs, and I have to get down to the lighthouse!"

Dumpy's engine gave a little cough.

"I know!" Charlie cried. "Let's use Dumpy! The pigs'll be safe in his dumper!"

"That's using the old noggin!" Pop-Up grinned.

One by one, the squealing pigs were rounded up and placed safely in the back of the little dump truck.

Pop-Up escorted the sodden Miss Morris to her front door and gave her his handkerchief. Big Red sprang into action, his flashing lights magnified by the teeming rain.

"**WOO-WOO-WOOO!**" he sang. "Never a dull moment!" And he led the convoy off toward the lighthouse.

As they were approaching the headland, Polly the Police Car went streaking past them.

"**WEE-OO, WEE-OO, WEE!**" she wailed. "When there's trouble, count on **MEE!**"

They arrived to find Lundy, the lighthouse keeper, in a state of great agitation.

"I just saw a flare at sea!" he was saying. "I think it's *Saucy Sue*. She was on her way in when the lightning struck!"

"She probably can't sight the harbor," said Fireman Tony.

"I'm worried she'll founder on the rocks," Lundy continued. "With no light and no horn, there's no way to bring her in!"

"The storm's going to last all night," added Police Sergeant Molly Mott. "Replacement parts won't get here till morning."

They huddled together, straining for a glimpse of the little trawler on the wild and wind-tossed water.

ZZZIP! Another zigzag of lightning slashed at the headland. Dumpy's headlights blinked on and off.

"That's it!" cried Charlie. "*We'll* be the lighthouse! If all the trucks flashed their lights together . . ."

". . . and *all* sounded their horns!" Pop-Up caught on immediately.

"We'd be bright enough and loud enough for *Saucy Sue* to find her way home!" Charlie finished.

"You know . . . it just might work!" said Lundy excitedly.

The trucks roared into action, and quickly lined up across the headland. Lundy stood in front of them, stopwatch in hand, and called out the code: "Four flashes, one long BEE-E-E-E-P!

Rest . . . and REPEAT!"

He raised his handkerchief, then waved it down, and the bright beams from the headlights pierced the darkness with precision timing. The horns trumpeted in unison, bouncing off the rocks and echoing out to sea.

There was no response.
The pigs in Dumpy's bed peered out with interest.

FLASH, FLASH, FLASH, FLASH, BEE-E-E-P! The
code rang out again. People and pigs waited anxiously for any sign
of the trawler in the driving rain.

"There she is!" yelled Charlie as *Saucy Sue*'s red and green
running lights suddenly appeared out of the darkness.

The little boat slid past the treacherous rocks, missing them by inches. **TOOT**-ing her thanks, she safely rounded the breakwater and headed into the harbor.

A great cheer went up, accompanied by squeals from the enthusiastic pigs.

All night long the storm raged. All night long the trucks kept their lighthouse vigil. Lundy was a hero, conducting his valiant crew in the pouring rain, fortified from time to time by Mrs. Barnes's hot soup.

"We'll remember this for years to come!" Pop-Up beamed proudly at Charlie as Dumpy lent his voice to the noisy chorus.

Finally, in the early hours of the dawn, the storm broke, and a watery sun appeared through the clouds.

Dumpy and his sleepy passengers **BEEP**ed farewell to their friends. As they drove off, they passed Trusty the Mail Truck, on his way to the headland with replacement parts for the lighthouse.

"**WOTTLE-WOTTLE-WOTTLE-WOT!**" Trusty wheezed. "Through hail and sleet and dead of night, your mail will reach you, come **WOT** might!"

The Pickwick pigs were returned safely to their farm.
Farmer Barnes put his arm around Charlie.

"This little truck really outdid himself," he said.
"We made quite a team, didn't we?"

"*Everyone* helped!" Charlie marveled.

Pop-Up smiled. "That's what friends are for!" he said.
"**BRROOOM, BRROOOM,**" Dumpy agreed softly.
And they all headed for home.

For Stephen, the dreamer, with all our love

Text and illustrations © 2002 by Dumpy, LLC.
Dumpy the Dump Truck is a trademark of Dumpy, LLC.
All rights reserved.
No part of this book may be reproduced or transmitted in any form or by any means, electronic or mechanical,
including photocopying, recording, or by any information storage and retrieval system, without written permission from the publisher.
For information address Hyperion Books for Children, 114 Fifth Avenue, New York, New York 10011-5690.
Printed in Hong Kong
This book is set in 18-point Cochin.
The artwork for each picture was prepared using watercolor and colored pencil.
First Edition
1 3 5 7 9 10 8 6 4 2
Library of Congress Cataloging-in-Publication data on file.
ISBN 0-7868-0742-3
Visit www.hyperionchildrensbooks.com